The Tale of Bella Brontosaurus

Terri Wiltshire

ILLUSTRATED BY
Rebecca Archer

Kingfisher Books

NEW YORK

Bella was having a
dreadful dinosaur-sized
awful day.

"What's this?"
she thundered.
"Someone has nibbled the
tastiest leaves from
my tree."
She stamped her feet.
Ker-Thump! Ker-Thump!

The ground shuddered
and the trees shivered.
"Who did this?" she bellowed.
But no one answered.

"What's this?" roared Bella. "Someone has turned my beautiful lake into a muddy mess." She stamped her feet. Ker-Thump! Ker-Thump!

The volcanoes rumbled
and pebbles crumbled.
"Who did this?" she shouted.
But no one answered.

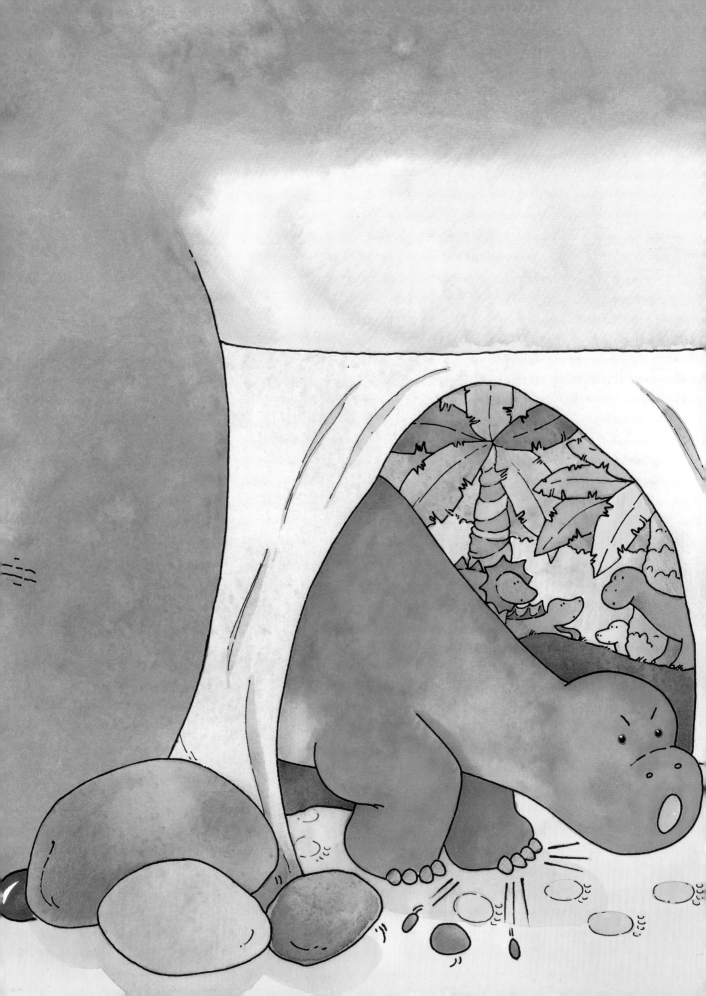

"What's this?"
screamed Bella.
"Someone has left dirty
footprints in my cave."
She stamped her feet.
Ker-Thump! Ker-Thump!

The mountains trembled
and boulders wobbled.
"Who did this?"
she shouted.
And a small voice said,
"I did."

"Why have you been nibbling my trees and swimming in my lake and resting in my cave?" Bella yelled.

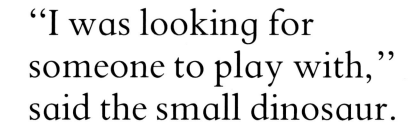

"I was looking for someone to play with," said the small dinosaur.

The other dinosaurs gasped.
Bella frowned.
Everyone held their breath.
Bella began to smile.

"I'll play with you," she said.
"A friend is just what I need."

And Bella and her
new friend played
Hop-and-Ker-Thump
together until the hills
rumbled and the water
rippled and the sky shook.

KINGFISHER BOOKS
Grisewood & Dempsey Inc.
95 Madison Avenue,
New York, New York 10016

First American edition 1993
2 4 6 8 10 9 7 5 3 1

Library of Congress Cataloging-in-Publication Data
Wiltshire, Terri
The tale of Bella Brontosaurus/Terri Wiltshire; [illustrated by]
Rebecca Archer — 1st American ed.
p. cm. — (Kingfisher foldouts)
Summary: Bella Brontosaurus has a bad day until she finds a new
friend. The cover folds out to provide a backdrop for the story.
1. Toy and movable books — Specimens. [1. Dinosaurs — Fiction.
2. Toy and movable books.] I. Archer, Rebecca, ill. II. Title.
III. Series.
PZ7.W6997Tab 1993
[E] — dc20 92-46250 CIP AC

ISBN 1-85697-857-5
Printed in Hong Kong